MARK PORTER of ARGORON

Published by Dark Titan Publishing. A division of Dark Titan Entertainment.

Also available in paperback.

Prodigious Worlds is a branch of Dark Titan Entertainment.

Paperback ISBN: 978-1-7369944-3-6
eBook ISBN: 978-1-7369944-4-3

darktitanentertainment.com

WORKS BY TY'RON W. C. ROBINSON II

BOOKS/SHORT STORIES

DARK TITAN UNIVERSE SAGA

MAIN SERIES

Dark Titan Knights
The Resistance Protocol
Tales of the Scattered
Tales of the Numinous
Day of Octagon
Crossbreed
Heaven's Called
The Oranos Imperative

Forthcoming

Underworld
Magicks and Mysticism
The Resistance vs. The
Enforcement Order

SPIN-OFFS

In A Glass of Dawn: The Casebook of
Travis Vail
Maveth: Bloodsport
The Curse of The Mutant-Thing

Forthcoming

Trail of Vengeance
War of The Thunder Gods
Maveth vs. The Swordman

ONE-SHOTS

Maveth, The Death-Bringer
Mystery of The Mutant-Thing
Shade & Switchblade
Retribution of Cain
The Mythologists
Ambush Bot
Kang-Zhu

COLLECTIONS

Dark Titan Omnibus: Volume 1
Dark Titan Omnibus: Volume 2
Dark Titan One-Shot Collection

THE HAUNTED CITY SAGA

The Legendary Warslinger: The Haunted City I
Battle of Astolat: A Haunted City Prequel (KOBO Exclusive)
Redemption of the Lost: The Haunted City II
Consequences of the Suffering: The Haunted City III (Forthcoming)

SYMBOLUM VENATORES

Symbolum Venatores: The Gabriel Kane Collection
Hod: A Symbolum Venatores Book
Symbolum Venatores: War of The Two Kingdoms
Symbolum Venatores: Elrad's Chronicles
Symbolum Venatores: Mystery of the Magician (Forthcoming)
Symbolum Venatores: Twilight of the Gods (Forthcoming)

EVERWAR UNIVERSE
EverWar Universe: Knights & Lords
EverWar Universe: The Damned Ones (Forthcoming)

PRODIGIOUS WORLDS
Mark Porter of Argoron
Raiders of Vanok (Forthcoming)
Praxus of Lithonia (Forthcoming)

FRIGHTENED! SERIES
Frightened!: The Beginning
Frightened!: The Light Sky (Forthcoming)

INSTINCTS SERIES
Lost in Shadows: Remastered
Instincts: Point Hope (Forthcoming)
Shadow in the Mirror: Instincts II (Forthcoming)

DARK TITAN'S THE DEAD DAYS
Accounts of The Dead Days
Brand New Day: The Dead Days I (Forthcoming)

OTHER BOOKS
The Book of The Elect
The Extended Age Omnibus
The Horde
The Eleventh Hour: A Chevah Mythos Story
The Supreme Pursuer: Darkness of the Hunt (Forthcoming)
Massacre in the Dusk (Forthcoming)

THE DARK TITAN AUDIO EXPERIENCE PODCAST
Season 1: Introductions
Season 2: In a Glass of Dawn
Season 2.5: Accounts of The Dead Days
Season 3: Battle For Astolat
Season 4: Hallow Sword: Cursed

MARK PORTER of ARGORON

TY'RON W. C. ROBINSON II

CONTENTS

CHAPTER 1: THE INCIDENT

United States Army Lieutenant, Mark Porter is currently on a mission to Roswell, New Mexico. His focus is keen as he traveled alone, listening to musical instrumentals. As he drove, his cell phone rings and he answers it.

"Lieutenant Porter." he said.

"Porter, this is General Dunlap." the caller said. "How far are you from the site?"

"I'm looking at it as we speak." Porter said.

Porter drove to the entrance gate, where two soldiers stood. They opened the gate , permitting him entry. Porter recognized the location, while still speaking with the General on the phone.

"General, I must ask, what is this place?"

"This is Area 51."

"Area 51." Porter intrigued. "I never thought I would be here."

"See you inside, Porter."

Porter hung up the phone, entering into the front entrance of the buildings. Area 51 had the appearance of a small city, with dozens of soldiers and officials moving throughout. Most of which are military soldiers and scientists. Porter stepped out of the car, heading towards the front doors layered with bulletproof glass. He entered, being greeted by soldiers. Porter took a left turn toward the elevator. Inside the elevator were two scientists.

"Excuse me, but are you Mark Porter?" one scientist asked.

"Yes I am."

"Its an honor to meet such a well-known Lieutenant." the other scientist said.

"Thank you."

The elevator had reached its destination floor. Porter is the first one to walk out, only to avoid the two scientists. Porter walked down a hallway and in the distance, he saw General Dunlap. Porter begins walking toward him. General Dunlap saw Porter coming down the hall near him.

"Porter, right on schedule."

"Yes sir, General."

Porter and General Dunlap entered another room. As they walked, Dunlap began telling Porter a few details to the secret operations being held within the facility. Porter took a guess to what it may be with only Dunlap smirking without saying a word.

"Porter, there are some rules that you must obey, since you're here."

"Ok, General. What are they?"

"You must not tell a single soul what you're about to see in this next room." Dunlap said. "If you do, we will have no choice but to rid you of the world."

"I see. Must be something very important."

"Important?" Dunlap said. "Try highly secretive. If anyone found out about this, the world will turn for the worst."

They reached the room and the metal door slowly slides open. The room was surrounded with military security. Little light was emitted into the room as the rest was covered in darkness. Porter gazed around, seeing scientists doing autopsies on unknown beings.

"General, what is going on here?" Porter asked.

"I'll tell you once we've reached our location."

Passing through the security, walking into yet another room. This room was lit up with plenty of light and wasn't nearly as shrouded in darkness like the other. Inside the room is a long table with a device sitting in the middle. Porter and Dunlap approached the table, looking at the device.

"Porter, this device you see here is able to transfer beings, human or not, to other worlds."

"Other worlds? Like planets?"

"Yes. Perhaps even dimensions are a possibility. Testing will only reveal how soon."

"How is that possible?" Porter asked. "Has it been tested?"

"Not yet. We're still awaiting an answer from the President."

They walked around the table, looking from all angles. The device was shiny, projecting a blue light which directed into the air. Porter slowly held his hand over the device before Dunlap snatched it from getting closer.

"You don't want to do something that you'll regret."

"Sorry, sir."

As they stood looking at the device, an alarm goes off. Porter and Dunlap look around. Dunlap ran toward the doors, questioning the security as to what triggered the alarm.

"What the hell's going on?!" Dunlap yelled.

"The base, sir, its under attack!" a soldier yelled.

"Porter, stay where you are!"

He pulled out his pistol, looking outside the door. From the outside, he saw soldiers and scientists being attacked by an unknown force. The opposing force appeared to have tentacles, while wearing peculiar white robes with long white hair extending to their lower back. Dunlap glared out of the glass window of the door, staring at them, watching them kill the soldiers and scientists. Gunshots are heard from the outside, but they're dying left and right.

Porter approached toward the door, but is stopped by Dunlap, who commanded Porter to stay by the table.

"General, what's going on?!"

"Sit tight, Lieutenant!" Dunlap said. "We're in for a show."

Dunlap backed from the door as it bursts open. He began shooting at the beings, but the gunshots have no effect. Porter takes out his revolver and shoots one of the beings in the head, which kills it. Dunlap looks at Porter, astounded.

"Try that, General."

"I surely will."

They both begin shooting the beings that are coming into the room through the damaged door. They aim for the head and shoot them directly there. They've killed the beings and look at each other. Both astounded and calm.

"Good job, Lieutenant."

"Same to you, General."

They shook hands, but from the ceiling a bright light shines down on them and Porter pushes Dunlap out of the way and a loud bang is heard with a large flash of light, nearly blinding Dunlap. The light fades away and Dunlap looks around for Porter.

"Porter?" Dunlap spoke. "Porter?!"

Dunlap looks around and realizes that Porter is nowhere in sight, but he also realized that the device's light is now dim, which before it was bright. He now knows that someone has happened to Porter.

Porter, who's opening his eyes, realizes that he's in a desert. He looks and stands up, brushing the dirt off of his uniform. He walks around the area, looking around at it surroundings.

"Where the hell am I?"

CHAPTER 2: CAPTIVE FOREIGNER

He continued walking, although realizing that he can move faster and jump higher than usual. Knowing now something isn't quite right. He continued to move ahead, but in front of him, he sees something running towards him. He tries to get a closer look and he sees that they looked human. He begins running the other direction, but is shot down by a bow and arrow. Porter lays on the ground as the beings get closer to him. He now hears silence, but the beings are surrounding him.

The beings appeared to be humans, yet there was a difference to them. Their skin was darker and their bodies were toned. They stared down Porter as he glared at them. They spoke to each other in an unknown language that Porter couldn't understand. He stood up, staggering from the arrow wound, stepping back from the beings and points to the one wearing white fur over his shoulders. His stature gave Porter to belief to be the general.

"You, where am I? Tell me where the hell I am?!"

The humanoids looked at Porter, their thoughts ponder if he's not from their world. One approached Porter and looks at him from all angles and stands back with his group. Porter stares at the group, reaching for his revolver, but he doesn't have it. He looks at what he perceived to be the humanoids' general and saw he had his revolver.

"How did you get that?!" Porter asked with rage. "Where am I?!"

Porter walked over to the beings, but he's knocked unconscious by one of their punches. They dragged him back to their location, locking him up. Hours later, Porter awakens and is now chained to a rock with no way out. He sees the beings from before, but this time, there's more. Porter begins thinking that he may not be on Earth anymore. He know believes that he's somewhere else, somewhere unknown.

Porter tried to break himself out of the chains, but he's too tired and weary to do so. He looks around as he's surrounded by dirt and feces. He continues to look around to find an object that could break him out of the chains. He doesn't find any tools that he could use, so he sits in the dungeon through the entire night. The next day, he awakens and sees himself surrounded by the tall, green beings. One in particular, releases him of the chains and helps him up, Porter stares at the being and looks into its eyes.

"What are you?" Porter asked.

"We are the Micrans." The being said. "Warriors of Argoron."

"What...? Argoron? Where am I?"

"You are on Argoron, stranger."

"Argoron?' Porter said. 'Where is that? I've never heard of Argoron.'

"If you're not from here, then, where do you come from?.' The being said. "What is your origin?"

"I'm not understanding what you mean? Where exactly am I?"

"You're on Argoron. A planet in the vastness of the stars."

"Argoron?" Porter questioned. "No. I was just in New Mexico."

"Where do you come from? Truly?"

"My name is Mark Porter." Porter said. "."

From the entrance came the leader of this particular warrior clan, Saban Jai. Saban walked toward and stood in front of Porter. Porter stared, not knowing what to expect.

"Mark Porter." Saban said. "How can you be from Jagoron?"

"What? No, I'm from Earth, not Jagoron? What is a Jagoron?"

"That is what I said, Mark Porter of Jagoron The world you come from is called Jagoron in this land. To your species, the earth-walkers, Jagoron is called Earth."

Porter sat confused. The Micrans didn't know what to make of his reaction. Saban didn't bother with him, rallying the others to bring him to the carriage. The carriage seemed to be made of a reddish wood as were the wheels, decorated with spears and red flags with no markings. Two of the Micrans carried Porter into the carriage, which was pulled by two eight-legged creatures. Which Porter saw them, he immediately thought them to be horses. However, he spotted they each had two tails and two sets of eyes on both sides. Speaking the word, Saban chuckled.

"Moreks." Saban said. "That's what they are. The fastest beasts in all of Argoron."

Saban jumped into the front of the carriage, gaining control over the horses as they rode off from the vast desert toward the massive metropolitan city as they approached the gates of the city of *Taranopolis*, as the inhabitants called it. Porter took a look outside of the carriage, seeing the massive city with its pointed skyscrapers and layered structures. The vehicles which moved throughout the city were a mix of the carriage and anti-gravity ships. The ships appeared to have four sets of transparent wings in the colors of rubies. The sky above the city was orange with a hint of red. The city was surrounded by red flags, flowing calmly with the wind throughout the city as the temperature was warm enough to have the people dressed in light clothing. Some even glanced at Porter, seeing his attire. From there, Porter knew he was out of place, especially when glancing upward toward the ships.

"Where am I?" Porter asked himself.

The carriage stopped in front of the city's palace. The Micrans stood by the carriage door, dragging Porter to the outside as they entered the palace. Porter stood on his feet, being held by two

Micran soldiers, walking toward what he guessed was the throne room. In the room, Porter saw three chairs. Two were empty and the center one was full as there was a man sitting, speaking with another man. The man standing up had the wings of a dragon folded on his back and claws for fingers. Dressed in armored leather. The man sitting down was decked in armor, linen, and fur. On his head sat a crown made of what appeared to be gold or bronze. Porter couldn't make out any of it, yet, he knew they were royalty in their own way.

"You know why I've come and visited you, my lord."

"Yes, I am aware of your need for warriors. As of right now, there aren't many who are at my disposal for combat."

"What of your prisoners? What use will you have for them other than wasting away behind cell doors?"

The one in the chair nodded, rubbing his chin.

"You have a point."

They looked toward the entrance, seeing the Micrans carrying Porter. The man standing pointed and his yellow eyes widen. The man in the seat stood up, glaring toward the Micran warriors and the prisoner they held.

"A new prisoner?"

"My lord." Saban said, kneeling. "We have another prisoner in need of interrogation."

The man stared at Porter, seeing his clothing and his tone. He was uncertain of Porter's ethnicity to his own and the others around him. He turned back to Saban, raising his hand, giving him the order to stand.

"And what has this man done and what is he wearing?"

"We're not sure, sire. He was dressed in this manner when we found him."

"And where did you find him?"

"Out in the wilderness. He appeared dazed. Confused you might say. He was speaking strangely, so we brought him here. To

8

get more answers. If you request it, my king."

The King nodded.

"Very well. Take him to the room. Ivo will be there to get any answers we may need."

"And what of him after you received your answers?" The other man said.

"When the time comes, I will call to you, Wyvern King. Right now, best you return to your domain. Prepare your warriors for the entertainment of the masses."

"I will keep my eyes and ears open."

The Wyvern King's wings buckled as he nodded his head, walking toward the exit. The King looked back, seeing Saban and the warriors leading Porter into the interrogation room. He sighed as he sat down and from the entrance arrived a young woman, dressed in a silver dress and long reddish-orange hair. She bowed before the king and he smiled.

"My daughter. I see you've returned from your journey."

"I have, father. I also have some news regarding the people of the city."

"News? What kind of news?"

"The people are aware of the coming war with the Celedians."

"And how do they know this?"

"Some have described a strange man coming into the city, warning them of the war and giving them the choice to choose which side they're on."

"A speaker of war in my city." The King said. "I see I must find him. Or, perhaps Saban has already brought him in."

The Princess wasn't sure what her father had meant. He chuckled and stood up, walking toward his daughter.

"Let me handle the matters of war. You must prepare for a wedding. Saban is a good man and a future leader."

"I... I understand."

The King looked at his daughter as she let out a small smile.

9

"I have other matters to attend to. Make sure you keep yourself protected when you're out in the city."

"The guardsmen will stand by me."

"Good, my Arribel."

CHAPTER 3: WHO ARE YOU?

Porter struggled against the strength of the two Micrans as they chained his wrists to the wall before exiting. Porter stared quietly, hearing footsteps approaching the cell. The door had opened for Porter to glance at two other warriors and a peculiar following the middle. He stood about the height of Porter, but he was much older as his white hair could attest.

"Who are you?"

"What?" Porter said slowly.

"Who are you? What is your name?"

"My name is Mark Porter."

"Mark Porter." Ivo said. "Strange name. never heard of such a one. Tell me, Mark Porter, where are you from?"

"I'm not from here. So, that's a start."

"Your name tells me all I need to know. Why have you come here, Mark Porter? Are you a spy for the Celedians? The Ceruleanians? Orgons, perhaps?"

"What are you talking about? I'm not from this place. "

"Your physical tells the tale. You're a warrior."

"I'm a soldier. A lieutenant."

"Convenient." Ivo chuckled. "And you've come here for what purpose other than being a spy or an invader?"

"I am not an invader nor am I some kind of spy. I didn't come here on my own accord. It's hard to explain. Even for myself. The place I come from is Earth. Earth is my home."

"Earth? You speak of Jagoron, the blue world where the waters move across the grounds."

"I guess you can detail it as much."

"Who sent you here?"

"I don't know."

"Then, start with something for me to go along. To understand your plight."

Porter sighed, waving his hands slight in a non-caring manner, yet, Porter began to tell Ivo of the encounter in Area 51, the ambush, and the instant transportation. Ivo listened closely to every word Porter had spoken. Once Porter had come to the conclusion of his sudden appearance in the desert, Ivo ceased him.

"You were brought here."

"Yes. But, I'm not sure by what or how."

"What is it you truly desire at this moment?"

"To be out of these chains and to be sent back home."

Ivo chuckled.

"There will be a time for that. Getting you back home however, is a tricky obstacle. For if you do not know how you came to Argoron, how does it make sense for you to find your way back."

"I saw the ships you people have. They're far beyond what I've seen. Now, I can take one of them and fly it back to Earth. A safe passage to get home."

"Enough." Ivo said, silencing Porter. "Our customs are far different than your kind. For one to achieve the freedom which one craves, they must earn it and win it."

"Win it? I'm not understanding."

"Combat. A trial to test your strength. To learn your endurance. Mentally. Physically. Spiritually. Only then will we and yourself see the conclusion to the whole matter."

"Are you telling me I must fight to get home?"

"Yes."

Porter sighed. Hanging his head low. He thought for a moment if this was only a dream. A hallucination, yet, with the small pain he felt in his legs, he knew it was real. All of it.

"I'm sorry. But, I am not going to be treated as some sort of amusement to you and your people here. I demand to be sent home."

Ivo turned back and walked toward the cell door. He opened it before taking a look back at Porter. Measuring him with a gaze.

"Your freedom demands on your fighting spirit. I hope you have one."

Ivo exited the cell, calling over a Micran guard. Ivo signaled the guard to keep watch of Porter's cell for the remainder of the day and throughout the night. Several hours later, nightfall fell over Taranopolis and the city was sleep. The sky which as glowing red had become as dark with glares and glistens of a peculiar bluish hue. Porter sat inside his cell. Barely ate the food they delivered to him. He looked over toward the guard sitting at the door. With the faint light shining from the window above him, Porter caught the glimpse of a key. Believing the key to be the only way out of his cell. Porter made a move, but remembered his wrists were attached to chains embedded into the concrete wall.

"Hey." Porter whispered. "Hey."

The guard jolted a bit, no movement afterwards. Porter sighed as he looked around the cell for something. Anything to get the guard's attention. Porter thought and glanced over to his left, seeing the tray of food. His eyes moved from the tray to the guard. Porter swiped his foot, kicking the tray against the cell doors, rattling up the guard as he jumped up with a sword in hand. Porter saw the blade.

"What's going on in there?" The guard asked.

"Water." Porter said. " I need water."

"Water? Where do you see any water?"

"To drink. I need something to drink."

The guard sighed and walked off, leaving Porter waiting. Unsure of what he could've waited for, the guard had returned, holding a small flask in his hand. He opened the cell door and entered, putting the flask on the ground as he unlocked the cuff from Porter's right wrist from the chain. Porter sighed and paused, quickly snatching he flask and smashing it into the guard's face before kicking the guard in the throat and stomping on his head. The helmet which the guard had word was cracked on the side. Porter looked to the guard's hand, seeing the key. He grabbed it and unruffled his left wrist. Being free from the wall, Porter grabbed the chest plate and helmet of the guard. Taking the sword last as he made his escape from the cell. Porter moved through the corridors quietly, avoiding other guards and even those who were playing a game of *L'agh*. In the distance, Porter saw the moonlight peaking from a doorway. Porter reached the door and found himself staring at the outside toward the vast desert. He sighed, knowing if he wanted to escape, going back into the desert was his only option. Porter made his move and ran out into the desert with only Argoron's moon as his source of direction.

CHAPTER 4: THE FLYING MEN

Porter had went afar out into the desert, he even glanced back and could only see the tips from the skyscrapers which stood in Taranopolis. Gasping for breath and of thirst, Porter continued walking. Even in the chilling cold. The air was almost below freezing to Porter's understanding. As he walked, he took a gaze up into the sky, seeing the peaking sun hovering behind a set of clouds. The heat began o rise throughout the desert sands as Porter continues trekking along the dunes around him. No sign of life. No animals. No plants. Porter walked alone in the desert.

From there, he came to a stop at what he believed to be a entry into some kind of cavern. Exhaling from the long walk, Porter approached the entry point, discovering the entrance into a small cave. He stepped forward to the cave and let out a faint shout. Nothing responded. He took the time to sit down and relax himself. He closed his eyes and calmly breathed. Afterwards, he heard what he believed to be something running within the cavern. Using his remaining strength to stand, Porter entered the cavern deeper and found a small pond which was set by a waterfall within the cavern. Pleased, Porter ran over into the pond, soaking himself in the water. He went and drank from the waterfall. In a strangeness to him, the water was cool. Near icy.

"Where does this water come from in a place such as this?" Porter thought to himself.

Taking several minutes to relax himself within the pond. He

stepped from it and returned to the entry point. Once he saw the sand in the distance, he caught three shadows in the sand. Hearing the wind above him. Porter ran out to see what was in the air and what he had seen were the wyvern men. Half-man and half-wyvern. Their bodies from their head to their waist were similar to a man. Yet, their legs and wings were of wyverns. Porter went and hid in the cavern, but one of the wyvern men caught him as he sat back against the rock wall. The wyvern man flew down to the cavern as Porter remained silent.

"Whatever you are," The wyvern man said. "Come out and face us."

Porter sighed in regret and slowly took his steps out of the cavern for the wyvern man to see. Unknown to Porter of the wyvern man's height. He stood over Porter by nine-feet and a half. The second wyvern man flew down, standing besides his partner as they stared at Porter. Seeing his garb. They were dumfounded.

"You're a strange one."

"I'm strange?" Porter said. "Look at the two of you. Hybrid beasts."

"What do they call you?" The wyvern man asked.

"My name?"

"Do you have one?"

"Mark Porter."

"Very well, Mark Porter. Myself and my colleague are elite soldiers for the Wyvern King. This cavern and the water within belong to him and him alone."

Porter chuckled.

"You're saying this king of yours owns this?"

"Precisely. As of this moment, you are trespassing."

"Listen, this is the best place I've come to so far on this planet or wherever the hell I am. Now, I am going to give the two of you to the count of three to leave me alone. Go fly up and bother someone else."

"You are not authorized to give us orders."

"I just did. What are you going to do with them?"

The second wyvern man looked over to his partner. Pointing at Porter's body. Noticing his demeanor and attitude. The first wyvern man took notice and nodded before turning his gaze toward Porter.

"If you won't leave our king's cave, then we must take you to him."

Porter balled his fists and clashed them. Standing tall before the wyvern men. They looked to one another and only came to a silent agreement. Before Porter to throw a punch, the wyvern men tackled him, stomping him into the sand. Porter tried to block the stomps with his arms, but one of the stomps collided with his head and chest, knocking him inconspicuous. Once the wyvern men knew of Porter's current status, they agreed to take him and they did. Carrying him in the air as they flew back to their place of origin.

CHAPTER 5: FINDING THE WARRIOR

Within Taranopolis the same day and hour, the guards searched the city searching for Porter under the orders of King R'akl. The guards returned to him, informing him of Porter's disappearance and lack of trace in the city region. King R'akl wondered how Porter made his escape in the night and several guards approached the king, detailing in of the discovery of a dead guard in the cell where Porter was kept. With murder being the case, R'akl called for a manhunt on Porter to be searched out and arrested on sight. The guards took in the king's command and headed out to find Porter even outside the city region. Princess Lola approached her father with caution, asking for alternative ways to find Porter. But, the king did not want to hear a word from his daughter regarding the foreign prisoner.

"What if he comes across the others? Like The Wyvern King?"

"If he does come across the Wyvern King, then the Wyvern King will bring him back to us. He knows our ways and if he doesn't want Micran warriors on his doorstep, then, he will return what is ours without haste."

"You know the Wyvern kind just as much as the rest of us. They will take whatever they can and use it for their own cause. If they come across him, they will use him against your kingdom. Against all of us under your command.

"Enough, my daughter." R'akl yelled. "Leave such matters to me. Right now, you should be concerning yourself with your upcoming marriage to Saban Jai. Focus on that and leave the duties of warfare to me. For these will become such matters for Saban when he is king."

"Yes, father." Lola replied, bowing before her father as she took her leave.

Leaving the palace, Lola commanded two guards to bring her one of the traveller-chariots. She instructed them to leave outside of the city gates. Unknown to her reasoning, they did not bother to question her, for she is the king's daughter and future wife to Saban Jai. Obeying her word, Lola arrived outside the gates, seeing the chariots. She stepped onto the chariot as one of her handmaidens approached. Getting on the chariot as well.

"What are you doing?" Lola asked.

"I'm coming with you. No need for you to travel out there alone."

"If we're caught, you'll be in serious trouble. Possibly banishment or death."

"I will do what I must for the future queen."

Lola nodded with uncertainty as they rode off into the desert. While riding in the desert, the handmaiden, who's name was Serai asked Lola where they were heading. Lola informed Serai she was heading to the landmass of the Hibarian Forest. Serai questioned why would Lola seek help inside the deep forest, Lola only responded by detailing they will need to speak to the dwellers who live within and without the forest.

After some time had passed, Lola looked ahead, seeing the palm-like trees in the distance. The Hibarian Forest was near. A land parallel to the desert. Lush with grass, flowing water and many, many trees. Trees standing nearly the height of Taranopolis' skyscrapers. Nearing the entrance to the forest, they are stopped by two figures. Standing over ten-feet tall. Their skin

19

was as green as the grass and their eyes were as golden as the sand. Brute physiques and rough demeanors. Lola knew what they were as she raised her hands in the midst of them aiming their weapons toward her.

"I come not to bring trouble. I am looking for someone. Perhaps you might have seen him."

"We do not understand what you speak of."

"There was a prison who escaped Taranopolis. I have come to ask if you've seen the man."

"We've seen no Micran."

"This man is not a Micran. He is something else. Beyond Argoron.

From the trees behind the guards came forward another one of their kind, yet covered in fur and jewelry. The two guards knelt down before him.

"Princess Arribel. Why have you come to our domain?"

"Lord Tartarus Kai. I have come to speak to you and your kind on an urgent request."

"How urgent is this request you have brought?"

"There was a man who was taken captive by my father. He escaped and fled. Most likely out in the desert. I have come to ask if you have seen this man."

Tartarus nodded, rubbing his chin. He shrugged shoulders without question. Just calm.

"I have not come across a Micran. Nor would one of them step foot near this forest by any means."

"As I told your guardsmen, this man is not a Micran. He's not from Argoron. He's from someplace else."

"Then, where did this prisoner originate from? The stars above? A planet far from our own?"

"Those are a possibility." Lola said. "I just need to find him before-"

"Before the Wyvern King has him, right?"

"Yes."

"Well, for all that it's worth, the Wyvern King probably has the prisoner by now. We have not seen this man anywhere near the forest."

Lola sighed with worry as Serai went to calm her. Tartarus stepped forward, looking down at the princess. He saw she had concern for the prisoner, which he deemed strange considering she didn't not fully know the origins or personality of the prisoner. However, he saw that she could see what would come to pass if Porter had been taken by the Wyvern King and what he could be used for. Being the Wyvern King is an adversary to his own ruler ship, Tartarus laid his hand on Lola's shoulder.

"I have an offer for you."

"Which is?"

"Sense the prisoner did not come across this region and it is more than likely the Wyvern King has taken him to Alderan, I will lend you two of my warriors to accompany you in your search."

"Um, I'm not sure what to say to that."

"No need. The better the Wyvern King doesn't have an upper hand the better."

"And what will you do if my father discovers you helped me?"

"Then, I will have a share of words with your father. Respectfully. No need for Micrans to fight against Celedians while the Wyvern kind continue to roam above our heads like *turuls*."

Lola agreed as the two Celedians stepped onto her chariot and they rode off with Tartarus watching as he turned back and entered the forest.

Elsewhere, the Wyvern Men flew down over a city. The city was complete made of mud bricks, detailed in the sand of the desert. The wyvern men carried Porter as they entered into a huge kingdom, the kingdom of Alderan. Overseen by the Wyvern King.

21

The city was surrounded by full-grown wyverns hovering and flying across the sky. Inside the kingdom, the others who dwelled there appeared to be part-human and part-wyvern themselves with only a slight few being completely humanlike or wyvern-like. They took Porter into the rock-layered palace. Inside, they set Porter on the ground and stood beside him. Porter remained unconsciousness as he was overseen by other wyvern men. Dressed in armor from their heads to their feet..

"Is this the man you saw, my king?" one of the wyvern men asked.

"Why yes." said the Wyvern King as he entered the palace. "This is the one who caught my eyes."

Porter's body jolted as he began to regain consciousness. Raising his head slowly, finding himself surrounded by wyvern men and standing before him, the Wyvern King. Porter raised up quickly, attempting to stand on his feet as the wyvern men rushed over, holding him down on his knees with their hands pressing against his shoulders.

"No need to worry, strange man." The Wyvern King said. "You'll soon get the answers you seek."

Porter stared at the Wyvern King as he sat down in his throne seat, sitting with one leg stretched out and a sinister grin on his face. His eyes piercing like a dragon and his claws sharp both on his hands and feet. His skin was rough and darker than the sands.. Porter staggered as he continued to try and stand up.

"Who are you?" Porter asked.

"I am your new lord and master, I am the Wyvern King."

"The Wyvern King. Where the hell am I?"

"You're in the city of Alderan. My domain of ruler-ship. Where else could you be?"

"I demand my exit. I demand to return home."

"Oh, you wish to return to Taranopolis?"

"Taranopolis? I'm not from this place. This planet. I want to return to Earth."

The Wyvern King paused, standing up from his seat, steeping down the stairs toward Porter. The King inched closer to get a better look at Porter. Seeing his skin, his hair, and his eyes. The wyvern King scoffed.

"You're telling me you're from the world beyond?"

"the world beyond? I'm from the planet called Earth."

"My lord," a wyvern men said. "I believe he speaks of the world of Jagoron."

"Jagoron. Ah, the place where the waters outnumber the land. You come from such a place?"

"I do and I wish to return there."

"Well, I'm not sure how you ended up here. But, I am most definitely unsure how you'll return there."

"You cannot keep me here." Porter said. "I am not some prisoner."

"I beg to differ. The Wyvern King rebutted. "You see, when I saw you back in Taranopolis, the Micrans were bringing you in as their prisoner. In between then and now, you somehow made your escape and now, you're here in my city. In my kingdom. Therefore, you and now my prisoner and the only way those who are granted their leave from my kingdom is through combat."

"Combat?"

"If you can survive the Pit, you can have your freedom."

"I'm not a gladiator." Porter said. "I do not fight for sport!"

"You are one now. Survive my Pit. Entertain my guests and freedom will be yours."

The Wyvern King commanded his soldiers to take Porter to the dungeons. They stand Porter on his feet and Porter lunged toward the King with his fists, the King, using his own weight, pushed himself back as his wings emerged, taking up much of the space surrounding the throne. Terror had slithered into Porter as he eyes widen from the wingspan. The Wyvern King rushed toward Porter, punching him in the face. Porter fell to his knees from the sharpening blow.

"Take this specimen to the dungeons, now." the Wyvern King said.

"Yes, my king."

CHAPTER 6: TO WIN BATTLES IS TO WIN WARS

They drug Porter to the dungeons, throwing him in and shutting the doors. Porter rushed to his feet, taking a gander around the dungeon, seeing no one else inside with him. He approached the steel doors and gazed out, seeing a group of wyvern men standing and talking with one another. Unable to make out their conversation, he heard a thud against the wall on the opposite side of the dungeon. From there came muffled sounds of screams and beatings. The wyvern men turned back, looking toward the opposite dungeon and rushed over, opening the door. Porter could hear the wyvern men yelling and their wings flapping. Afterwards was only silence as the wyvern men stepped out from the dungeon, carrying a prisoner dressed in golden armor. Porter looked, seeing the prisoner appeared to be a human.

"What have you done to him?" Porter questioned.

"Quiet, slave. We do not answer to you."

"He's a human. You're keeping humans as slaves for what?"

"You ask why you're here? Because the audience needs entertainment. Today, is your attempt at giving it to them. By the orders of our king."

A loud horn roared across the sky. Porter gazed up and so did the two wyvern men. They looked to each other before turning toward Porter. One of them approached the door, unlocking it as the other entered the dungeon, fighting off Porter as they dragged him out and into another room. This room was full of other soldiers. Warriors from other lands outside of Alderan. Porter looked at them. Seeing the appeared to be human to his understanding. However, they only stared at him with confusion and strangeness. One of the gladiators stepped forward. A rugged-looking man. He stood over Porter by three feet. His stern demeanor proved he had been in Alderan for quite some time. Staring Porter in the eyes.

"The hell are you supposed to be?" He said, measuring Porter. "You're no Azurian."

"Get out of my face." Porter replied. "Before you end up on the ground."

"Or what? You'll kill me?" The gladiator chuckled. "Seeing as how we're all here to die anyway."

One of the wyvern men pointed toward Porter, demanding he remove his clothing. Porter disagreed, declaring he will keep on his uniform. The wyvern men rushed to him, stripping away his clothing. They left him naked as he looked around for something to cover himself with. One of the gladiators tossed him a tunic, which was detailed in its blood-red appearance with a golden sash. Porter put on the tunic as the wyvern men presented to him two golden leather gauntlets for his forearms. One of the gladiators tossed him a pair of boots with a leather-like appearance. However, when Porter touched them, the leather seemed unusual.

"What's this made of?"

"Enfield hide." the gladiator replied.

"Enfield?"

"They're very rare around these regions. Strong, brute creatures. You'll run in terror if you ever see them."

Porter nodded.

"I understand your concern."

Porter put on the boots when a wyvern man stood before him, holding a chest piece. He tossed it to Porter, commanding he put on he chest piece. Porter looked at the armor, feeling its ruggedness and its smoothness. Porter had asked if the armor had been previously used, only to receive the answer the armor belonged to a gladiator who was killed in battle several days prior. Porter looked at the center of the chest piece, noticing an insignia.

"What does this mean?"

"It means a stranger across worlds." The gladiator told him.

"Must mean the one who wore this came from another world." Porter said.

"He did. The place called Vanagon."

"Vanagon?"

"The second world from the distance of the Great Sun."

"Venus." Porter said quietly to himself.

Standing by the entry point of the armory and preparation room were two larger wyvern men. Both carried spears. They rallied the gladiators and Porter to prepare themselves for the fight ahead. Each of them formed an orderly line. Porter only looked on as they were searched and measured by the wyvern men. Seeing only their nods as the they were led toward the coliseum doors. The doors were over twenty-feet in height and the cheer of the crowd began to echo through them. Porter saw the gladiators were ready for the battle. Others were crying in fear. Porter kept himself calm as the gladiator he talked with stood beside him. Each of them were handed swords. Porter looked at the sword, seeing its sharpness and its light-weight.

"Strange material."

"Only found in the deepest parts of the Hibarian Forest."

"What's it made of?"

"Fallen star I was told. Possibly not."

"I see."

27

"Whatever you see out there, make sure not to give in to fear."

"What are you saying?" Porter questioned.

"What we're up against may seem terrifying to you. If you're like the others. For there are many beings and creatures which appear in these fights. All for the glory of sport."

"I'm not afraid. I just want to get out of here."

"Very well then. Survive the coliseum and you'll have it."

"I'm aware. Thanks for the tip. What is your name by the way?"

"Nakir. Yours?"

"Mark Porter."

One of the larger wyvern men stood by the door, glaring at the gladiators. He slammed the spear into the ground as the roar of the crowd soared behind him.

"Gladiators! Warriors of Alderan. This day, you will enter these gates and fight your way through a collage of beasts. A sea of soldiers from distant lands. I do not expect many of you to survive. For our king has gathered himself quite the nice spectacle for each of you to see. This fight will be one of the biggest ones Alderan has yet to put on and you all should be lucky to have participated within it. Now, I ask you. Do any of you seek your freedom? Then, if you do, you know what must be done. Survive and you'll have your freedom. Die and you'll have your freedom. If the gods permit it, of course."

The doors opened as the gladiators rushed out into the open field with only the sand of the grounds surrounding them. Porter and Nakir stood close as the other gladiators looked around at the crowd. Seeing the audience of a mixed-multitude. Porter was astonished by their presence.

"Didn't realize there were this many people living out here."

"Alderan is only a place for entertainment." Nakir said. "These people come from other lands. Distant from Taranopolis among others."

Porter looked straight ahead, seeing three other doors with wyvern men standing beside them. Porter pointed toward them as Nakir took notice.

"What's behind the doors?"

"The terror and dread which shall soon wash over the gladiators."

The Wyvern King walked out in the midst of the crowd, overseeing the grounds. Porter looked up, spotting him as he showered himself in the cheers. The Wyvern King sat down in a seat of his own. Similar to his throne. He raised his right hand toward the wyvern men at the first door. Signaling for it to open. They obeyed and the first door opened with all the gladiators prepared.

"Here we go." Nakir said.

Busting from the first door were tall, thin, and green looking creatures. Ten of them. They walked upright similar to humans, but they were not as they had shades of grass growing on their arms and legs and mushrooms on their shoulders, covered up by the armor around their torsos. No hair, long arms, legs, and their eyes were as white as snow. They roared together as they rushed toward the gladiators.

"The hell are they?" Porter wondered.

"Plant Men." Nakir answered. "Dwellers from the Hibarian Forest in the secluded lands."

"Noted."

The Plant Men collided with the gladiators. All fighting with swords. Some had shields which were scattered throughout the coliseum grounds. Porter saw one shield and ran over to grab it. Once he had it, a Plant Man dove over him with a sword and Porter blocked the attack with the shield and found an opening as he swiped the shield across the Plant Man's face and impaled him with the sword. Nakir battled a Plant Man, killing him by cutting off the legs and head. Porter looked round at the other gladiators, seeing them being overrun by the Plant Men. Porter couldn't take the sight as he intervened, crashing against the Plant Men with sword and shield. Nakir joined in and fought alongside him. So far, eight of the twenty prisoners were killed by the Plant Men. Porter and Nakir continued to fight as did the remaining prisoners. Inspired by Porter's relentlessness. Porter led the remaining gladiators against the last four Plant Men and they quickly decimated them with their swords. The Wyvern King stood up in awe and anger. His sight focused on Porter. He knew there was something to him and signaled for the second door to open, which came out were six-legged beasts. Two were hairless aside from the large manes around their necks. Four of them roaring and snarling. Porter stared as he saw hem walking out and the gladiators began to show signs of fear.

"Are those lions?" Porter asked.

"No." Nakir answered slowly. "Those are Beoths."

The Beoths roared in fury toward the gladiators. Mixing their ferocity with the cheers of the crowd. The gladiators banded together as the beoths charged toward them with their fangs and claws. One beoth leaped, lunging atop the gladiators as they held their shields overhead. Porter looked for an opening and slicked the back leg of the beoth as they shoved the large beast off the shields. A second beoth snatched one of the gladiators by his leg, dragging him and tossing him in the air as the others scattered around the area in sight of the beoths.

"Move with me!" Porter screamed.

The gladiators did not take heed to Porter's command as two beoths circled them. In front of Porter and Nikar jumped another beoth. Snarling as it stared into their eyes. Porter swiped the sword across the beast's face before kicking it in the nose. The beoth swiped with its pawed claws, scratching Porter in the leg. The beoth swiped again, knocking the shield to the ground. Nikar grabbed the shield as the beoth jumped over him. Nikar pressed against the beast's strength as it went for his head with its jaws. Porter saw Nikar on the ground and the beoth over him. He pressed on in pain from the scratch and leaped atop the beoth like a bull. The beast jumped around, trying to toss Porter from its back. Porter held his ground, raising the sword with one hand and impaling the beoth in its neck. One down as Porter helped Nikar to his feet.

"Thanks."

"No problem."

They looked on, seeing the gladiators stood no chance against the two circling them. They went to aid them before the other beoth jumped in front of them. This one more hairy than the last as Porter swiped the sword against it, but the hide and hair of the beoth was took thick for a strike. The beoth charged, slamming Porter into the arena walls as it chased Nikar. Porter stood up, rubbing his right shoulder, seeing the blood. He sighed as he made a run toward Nikar. Nikar dodged a paw swipe as Porter jumped on top of the beoth in similar fashion. The crowd savored all they were witnessing as did the Wyvern King. Porter held the sword, impaling the beoth in its neck, but the hair and hide were too durable.

"Dammit!" Porter shouted. "What are we going to do now?!"

Nikar stood, thinking. He looked over to the walls, seeing on the ground a long chain. Running over, he grabbed the chain and smelled it. Recognizing what material it was made of and he tossed it toward Porter. Porter caught the chain with his left hand as his right was occupied by the sword. The beoth leaped, tossing Porter from its back. Nikar ran toward Porter as the beoth charged at them both. Porter held the chain and told Nikar to stand back. Nikar moved as Porter stood up and wrapped the chain around the beoth's neck and pulled it back from the charge. The beoth's neck had snapped from the sudden strength of Porter, which startled Nikar and the crowd. Even the Wyvern King was

31

intrigued. The beoth's body lumped into the sand as Porter looked at his hands and the chain.

"Where did that come from?"

"The other two!" Nikar yelled. "We need to finish them off!"

"Leave it to me." Porter answered. "Toss me the shield!"

Nikar grabbed the shield, tossing it toward Porter. He exhaled and ran toward the gladiators as they fought off the two beoths to a less result. Porter yelled for them to spread out and they followed his order. While the spread, they split up the two beasts, separating them from a distance. One was hairy and the other was hairless. Porter targeted the hairless one first by using the chain and pull its leg as he leaped over, stabbing it in the neck. Moving without haste, Porter used the chain to pull the final beoth, wrapping the chain around its neck and tossing it on its back. Porter looked,realizing the abdomen was not covered with hair nor was the skin thick. Porter jumped over the beoth and impaled the beast in its chest with the sword. The audience cheered as Porter whipped the chain back from the beoth's neck and stood in the middle of the area, looking at the audience. They began to applaud him. The other gladiators took notice and Nikar nodded.

"Ugh!" The Wyvern King said, standing up from his seat. "Give it up for Mark Porter!"

The audience cheered louder and chanted Porter's name. the Wyvern King grabbed a spear and threw it directly in front of Porter. Crashing into the sand within two feet of him. The Wyvern King pointed toward him and the other remaining gladiators.

"You have won this day. But, on the morrow, oh, it will be the day you shall die."

The Wyvern King swiped his hands as the wyvern men escorted Porter and the gladiators back to the dungeons. The night had settled and this time, Porter was kept in the dungeon with Nikar and the two spoke about their past before the arena.

Nikar told Porter he had come from a place in the southern region of Argoron. A place he hoped to see again. Opening up, Porter began to tell Nikar of his home world of Earth. Nikar paused.

"You come from Jagoron?"

"I do. I guess Jagoron is your language for Earth."

"How did you get here?"

"I don't know. That's what I'm trying to find out."

"Once you achieve your freedom, I'm sure the answers will come."

"I hope so."

Elsewhere, Lola, Serai, and the Celedians took a stop at one of the Celedian camps several miles near Alderan. Lola looked ahead, seeing the city lights as the cold air blew over them. Serai handed Lola a cloak, one decorated in the royal redness of Argoron.

"We were informed of an event which happened in the city early this day."

"What did they say?" Lola asked.

"They said the audience was intrigued by a man. A strange one. He defeated beoths with ease. They said his strength was beyond comprehension."

Lola paused. Nodding to her own thoughts.

"It's him. It has to be."

"We'll find out in the morning. Right now, it is best you rest as shall we."

In the dungeon, Porter looked on, seeing Nikar was asleep. The area was silent. More silent than any place he's been since he had been on Argoron. He smirked, dreaming of his return to Earth and what he will tell those of his current adventure. He closed his eyes and fell into a deep sleep.

CHAPTER 7: FREEDOM OR SLAVERY

The next morning, the wyvern men bolted into the dungeons, awakening Porter, Nikar, and the gladiators. They prepared themselves and gathered their weapons which sat at the entry point of the arena. Porter listened as he heard the roaring crowd once again. The doors had opened and they went out. The Wyvern King stepped forward, commanding with a shouting voice that they open all three doors. The wyvern men obeyed as the doors opened. What Porter and the gladiators saw terrified them. From the first door entered a pack of wyverns. They flew toward the gladiators and they were prepared. Their hands gripped the hilts of their swords. Porter whipped his chain as he held the sword in his right hand. From the second door had arrived gladiators, however these were different. They were more brute in size and their skin glistened with the sunlight. Even their height towered Porter and the others.

"Those are the warriors from the faraway land." Nikar said.

"What's their stats?" Porter questioned.

"They kill whatever pleases them. Killing is only a sport for them."

"Noted." Porter nodded.

The brute gladiators ran toward them with force. While they were making their way near them, Porter looked ahead at the third door and he could feel the trembling in the ground. Looking at the sand, seeing it rise up and fall. Nikar could feel the tremors as well and he stepped back, leaving Porter in confusion.

"He has them." Nikar said. "He caught them."

"Has who?" Porter questioned. "Caught what?"

From the third door walked out two great and powerful creatures. Standing over thirty-five feet in height and incredibly hairy. One was as white as snow. The other was as dark as coal. The creatures smashed their arms in the ground, roaring to the cheer of the crowd. Porter stared at them. Impressed by their height and size.

"Are those gorillas?" Porter said.

"No." Nikar answered. "They are the Beasts of the wilderness. The white one is the Hoary Beast. While the black one is the Ruin Beast. Both are creatures of great destruction."

"We have to survive this."

"How?"

"Leave it to me." Porter said. "We're getting out of here this day."

The Beasts charged into the battle as the gladiators fought the brutes. The wyverns flew overhead, striking whenever they found an opening in the crowded swordfight. Porter gazed up toward a wyvern, using the chain to snatch the creature from the air to the ground. Once the wyvern had fell, Porter rushed over and impaled the creatures. He continued the same tactics to the other wyverns, only for one of the brute gladiators to tackle him to the ground. Porter rolled out of the path from the gladiator's large mace. Nikar ran into the fight, slashing his sword across the gladiator's arm, cutting it off with the mace in hand. Porter nodded to Nikar as he decapitated the brute. The wyverns continued with their snapping jaws, grabbing gladiators from the ground and throwing them across the arena, only for them to be stomped on by the Beasts. Porter took on two of the brutes with Nikar at his side. The gladiators who remained were quickly killed by the wyverns and Beasts. Leaving only Porter and Nikar to fight for themselves. Seeing themselves outnumbered. Porter focused his movement, striking the last two brutes with the chain and slashing the wyverns in the air as he jumped. Showing his impressive skill. Skills he didn't know he had before. Surprising the audience as Nikar stabbed the brutes after they were struck by Porter's chain. Several of the wyverns landed on the ground, seeking to lung on Porter. The wyverns went to pounce and the Beasts behind them trampled them without notice. Staring at Porter and Nikar as their prize.

"This is the day they die." The Wyvern King uttered.

Porter and the Hoary Beast come face-to-face. Porter jumped across the Beast to get a better shot with the sword, however the Beast took notice of the chain and snatched it, jerking Porter from the air, swinging him around until he is slammed into the sand as the Ruin Beast chases Nikar through the arena. Porter stood up, grabbing the chain with both hands, jerking it back towards him from the Hoary Beast. The Beast glared at Porter, huffing. The Hoary Beast slammed its fists into the sand, running toward Porter. Porter followed suit, charging toward the Hoary Beast himself with the sword in hand. Mark leaped into the air over the Beast's head, slashing the large creature down its back while landing a kick to the back of its head. The Beast stumbled from the slash and the kick fo only a few seconds as Porter landed on the ground. He turned around to face the Beast, twirling the chain. The Beast turned, staring at Porter. Porter grinned as he swung the chain with such force, it slapped the Beast in its head. The force of the chain whip caused the massive creature to fall and it laid in the sand with the audience in silence. Nikar looked over as he hid from the Ruin Beast in a corner, seeing the downed Hoary Beast. He smiled.

"He killed it!"

The Ruin Beast looked back, seeing the Hoary one dead. It roared with anger, preparing to charge toward Porter. Porter twirled the chain again, smirking. The Hoary Beast began to move slowly, attempting to raise itself up to its feet. Seeing the creature moving, Porter jumped on top of the creature's body and dug the sword through the throat, officially killing the creature. The Wyvern King glared with anger, yet signaled an applause for Porter's achievement. He began to clap and the audience followed suit. Porter turned to face the Wyvern King.

"I've taken down one of your Beast, Wyvern King." Porter yelled. "What more must I do to prove my freedom?!"

The Wyvern King raises his right arm as the wyvern men signaled the Ruin Beast's attention. Directing it toward Porter. The Beast roared and charged toward him. Porter paused for a moment, showing a faint sign of tiredness. Nikar stood up against the arena wall, cheering Porter on. He took notice and stood firm in the sand. Standing still in a fighting stance. Sword and chain both in his hands.

"Slaughter him!" The Wyvern King yelled.

The Ruin Beast looked down, seeing Nikar and proceeded to grab him from the wall. Porter ran over, pointing the sword toward the creature.

"Come at me!" Porter yelled toward the Ruin Beast. "Leave him alone!"

The Beast charged and once it reached closer, Porter jumped in the air, moving over the beast's head. He turned himself around in midair and raised the sword. The chain swiped against the creature's back and the sword itself was shoved through the back of its head, immediately killing it. The Wyvern King starts clapping and the audience begins clapping. Porter turns, facing the Wyvern King.

"I've taken down both your beasts, Wyvern King." Porter yelled. "What more must I do to prove my freedom is granted?!"

At the entrance to Alderan, Lola, Serai, and the Celedians arrive. Hearing the cheers of the crowd at the coliseum, they made haste toward it. Meanwhile, inside the arena, the Wyvern King stood up from his seat, walking down to the arena grounds to confront Porter. The audience was intrigued by their king's motives. Two wyvern men accompanied their king as he stepped foot on the sands drenched in the blood of his gladiators and creatures. The Wyvern King stood before Porter. Nikar sat back against one of the podiums attached to the arena walls.

"You seek your freedom." The Wyvern King asked.

"Yes. However, not only my own. But, his as well." Porter said, pointing toward Nikar.

The Wyvern King chuckled.

"I see. Very well. You have achieved your freedom. You are a free man. But, you have sought to gain the freedom of another. Therefore, there is one more fight you must endure."

Within the crowd, Lola, Serai, and the Celedians entered. Looking ahead as they saw Porter standing face-to-face with the Wyvern King. Lola wanted to go down and save him, but the Celedians resisted. Demanding she wait and watch what might come. Unsure of their ideas, she hesitated her own hastiness and sat down to watch.

"And what must I endure?"

"A final battle."

"Against what?" Porter asked. "More gladiators? More beasts?"

"No. Against me"

The wyvern men handed their king a spear. He stretched forth his wings, showing them to the audience, only to hear their cheers as they screamed his name. he grinned at the sound as Porter stepped back, gripping the chain and sword. The wyvern men on the ground flew away. Leaving their king and Porter on the field. Nikar stepped forward, only for Porter to raise his hand toward him. Nikar stepped back, nodding.

"Are you ready to die?" The Wyvern King asked.

"I won't die today." Porter answered.

The Wyvern King quickly attacked with the spear and his long tail covered in spikes. Porter deflected the spear and tail with the sword. Porter swiped the chain across the Wyvern King's chest, only to hit the armor. The Wyvern King laughed as he used the spear to trip Porter. He stood over him, holding the spear and Porter moved himself out of the weapon's path and wrapped the chain around the Wyvern King's leg, pulling him to the ground. He went to impale the Wyvern King to the ground, but the wings pulled him back and the tail of the King swiped Porter across his chest, knocking him to the ground. The audience was back and forth in reactions to the two dueling.

"You won't win this." The Wyvern King said.

"Keep fighting and we'll see."

The spear was raised, only for Porter to slash the sword across it, snapping it in half. He grabbed the end of the spear and shoved it in the side of the Wyvern King, causing him to stumble in his steps. Through the pain, he continued to fight, pulling the spear from his ribs and throwing it to the sand. He punched Porter across his face several times before grabbing him by his throat and slamming him. He set his foot over Porter's chest, raising his spiked tail above him.

"Give up."

"I will never."

Porter swiped the sword, cutting the ankle of the King. He kicked him back and stood up, using the chain to swipe against eh armor as it began to break from the constant blows. Porter had the Wyvern King down on his knees as he ripped the chest piece from him and impaled the sword. Gasps filled the air as Porter stared into the Wyvern King reptilian eyes.

"I am… not dead yet."

"Don't be sure of yourself."

Porter removed the sword and decapitated the Wyvern King. His body collapsed to the ground and the wyvern men around the arena let out a screeching yell. A yell in pain and agony. It was there, the Celedians busted into the arena, killing any wyvern men that did not fly away. At the entrance entered Tartarus Kai. He looked out at the audience and glanced down at the dead body of the Wyvern King.

"Citizens of Alderan! The tyrant is now dead! From this day forward, Alderan belongs to the Celedians!"

Porter approached Tartarus and nodded, holding the chain and sword.

"I think I'll be keeping these."

"Suit yourself. But, you have visitors who are expecting you."

Tartarus pointed toward the arena gates, seeing Lola standing. Porter looked at her and was unsure, yet, her beauty caught his gaze. Something he was not familiar with on this planet. Otherwise, Porter nodded to Nikar. Their freedoms were won as they exited the arena with the crowd cheering around them. In front, Lola approached them both, but her eyes were set on Porter.

CHAPTER 8: A HEROP

"I am Princess Lola Arribel of Taranopolis and I've been searching for you." Lola said.

"Ok, Princess." Porter replied. "Why, madam have you been searching for me?"

"Because you're needed. I saw you fight. Your skills. Your strength. You have what it takes to save us. To possibly save us all."

"I'm needed? Needed for what?"

"To help us stop what's coming."

"And what is coming?" Porter questioned.

"Her father, King R'akl has been betrayed by Saban Jai." Tartarus said.

Lola looked toward him, questioning how he would know of such information. Tartarus informed her that he set spies throughout Taranopolis and many of them received information of Saban's betrayal after making an alliance with the Wyvern King. Tartarus described the plans of Saban's intentions to have been revealed after he married Lola. Striking them at a most vulnerable position.

"Mr. Porter." Lola said, standing in front of him. "I need your help in this matter. Please, help my father and his people from Saban's betrayal."

"Porter looked down, nodded and gazed the surroundings. He shook his head in decline.

"I'm sorry. I just want to go home."

"Home?"

"Yes. Home. I'm not from this planet. Your political matters do not concern me."

"But, you're here on Argoron. Yet, there is something strange about you. You don't have the complexion to be an Argoronian."

"Of course not. I'm from Earth."

"Jagoron? Wait, how can you be from a world beyond ours?"

"I'm not sure myself. I seek to return there. I need to know how."

"I know of a way." Tartarus said.

"What is it?" Porter questioned. "Whatever it is you are."

"I am a Celedian. King of my kind. The name is Tartarus Kai."

"Mark Porter. Of Earth. Now, tell me what you know? How can I return home?"

"There is a portal caught in the rift of a pillar. A strong one."

"Where is this pillar?"

"Between the borders of Taranopolis and Alderan. If you take one of the travellers, you can make it there before nightfall."

"And if I go on foot?"

"Then, you'll be trekking in the dune sands for several days. Two at most."

Porter agreed to the offer as one of the Celedian warriors had presented him a traveller. Porter scoffed as he saw the vehicle. He walked around it, measuring it out.

"No tires?" Porter said.

"Tires?" Tartarus asked. "What is that?"

"They go on the bottom. Four on each side."

"This traveller needs no bottom compartments. Once you're inside, the controls will tell you what you must do."

"And how does it travel?"

"Anti-gravity."

42

"Interesting."

Porter entered the traveller as it powered up. The gear was in place and Porter was prepared to leave. Tartarus asked if Porter wanted a test run of the vehicle, yet Porter denied the request, preferring to learn as he goes. Tartarus understood and stepped back. Lola rushed toward the traveller, placing her hands on the door.

"You cannot just go along and leave us to a possible destruction."

"Look, madam. I'm sorry for what is happening in your home. But, I'm not from here. I'm just a foreigner and I want to return home."

"And will your conscience be content with your decision?"

Porter sighed. He gave Lola a stare.

"We'll see."

The traveller roared as it levitated over the ground. Porter jerked the wheel as he glared down at the ground, seeing the sand blow around the vehicle. Porter nodded to Tartarus and Lola as he rode away. Lola sighed in slight anger as Tartarus approached her.

"Don't worry yourself. There is a reason why myself and my warriors are here."

"What do you mean?"

"We cannot allow you and Serai to return to Taranopolis only to fall in Saban's hands. We'll accompany you and protect you and your father from Saban's army."

"And I guess you'll want my father to grant you something in return?"

"We'll talk about that after Saban is dealt with."

Lola agreed to Tartarus' assistance as he rallied all the Celedian warriors and they rode off toward Taranopolis.

CHAPTER 9: THE EARTHMAN'S CHOICE

Mark Porter rode out into the desert, gazing up toward the sun as he took note of its slow descending. He continued to ride and far out in the distance, Porter saw something standing in the middle of the sands. Coming up onto the object closer, Porter knew it was the pillar. Standing over twenty feet and carved out of what may have been a small mountain in the area. Porter reached the pillar and exited the traveller.

"What kind of structure is this?"

Porter looked around the pillar, finding a small pond and several small trees growing around it. From the pillar itself fell a waterfall. Porter wasn't sure how such an object or environment operate in the middle of the desert. Porter approached the waterfall and began hearing faint sounds of voices. The voices were familiar to him. Familiar to the point the began to call out names.

"General?"

Back at Taranopolis, Lola and Serai had made their return with Tartarus and the Celedian warriors behind them. Entering the city and startling the people, Lola made haste toward the palace and she entered just as her father was speaking with Saban.

She stooped herself in her steps with Serai by her side as they turned to see her. R'akl stood up from his throne and approached her as she knelt down. Saban was confused by her sudden appearance.

"We've been searching for you, my daughter."

"I'm sorry, father. But, I had to go out and find the prisoner."

"And did you?"

"Yes. He was in Alderan."

"Alderan." R'akl replied. "I knew it. I knew the Wyvern King would've taken him. He disobeyed my orders to keep him here. When I speak with him again, I will have much words for him."

"Father, the Wyvern King is dead."

Saban jolted and stepped forward with concern. R'akl only shook his head in hearing the words of the Wyvern Kong's death.

"What do you mean dead?" Saban questioned. "How do you know of this?"

"My daughter, who slew the Wyvern King of Alderan?"

"The prisoner. He called himself Mark Porter of Earth."

"Him." Saban said. "So, an earthman chooses to thwart Argoronian laws."

"You cannot blame him, Saban. He doesn't know our rules. How else could he have abided by them."

"We need to find this prisoner, my king. Before he comes here and tries to do the same to you. To me. To your daughter even."

"He had no intensions on killing me." Lola said.

"As of this moment." Saban replied. "My king, allow me and my warriors to go out into the dunes and find him. Bring him back and then, we can be rid of him."

Lola sighed, gathering their attention.

"There is something else, father. Something you must know."

"Speak it."

"The Celedians are here in he city."

"Celedians?!" Saban yelled. "Those savages!"

45

"Why are they here? And under who's orders did they receive permission?"

"They came to accompany me."

"Accompany you for what?"

"To protect you, father."

"Protect me?" R'akl replied with confusion. "Protect me from what?"

"Him." Lola said, pointing toward Saban.

R'akl turned toward Saban and they both gave looks of uncertainty. Layered with confusion. R'akl turned back to his daughter as Saban stood still, his eyes looking around the throne room.

"What proof do you have of this?"

Lola turned around as Tartarus Kai entered the throne room, ducking his head as he entered. Saban raised up his sword as he eyes widen toward the tall king. R'akl stood his ground, with his hand gently on the hilt of his blade. Tartarus stood before them both, yet, bowed his head before R'akl.

"King of Taranopolis. I did not come to make war."

"Why are you here, savage king?" Saban asked.

R'akl raised his hand, silencing Saban.

"Why have you accompanied my daughter back to her home?"

"I've placed several Celedian spies across your city for several months, king. I also had spies centered around Alderan and what they have informed me of, you must truly know. For it concerns the life of your daughter, your own, and your people."

"And what is this information?"

"Saban Jai is a traitor and a deceiver. He's been making plans alongside the Wyvern King to bring forth your demise. I told you daughter of this news and she has agreed to return here to tell you herself."

R'akl turned toward Saban. His eyes already speaking the truth.

46

"Why?" R'akl asked. "Why would you betray me? Betray all of us?"

Saban sighed, sheathing his sword and shrugging his shoulders.

"Because, it is time for all of Argoron to enter a new ruler-ship of power and might. In truth, my king, your rule has become weak. You grafted peace with this savage king and from there, you have only grown weaker. I knew it was the truth when the earthman appeared in the sands. There is other life out there. Other worlds in need of us. We have enough power to invade those planets and conquer them. Make them bow under Argoron laws and to worship our gods. Yet, you refuse. You want peace and nothing else."

"So, you sought to marry my daughter only to bring forth your plans of conquest?"

"I did. I have no reason to lie."

"It was never about love?"

"My king, it never was. Besides, you daughter is a beautiful woman. But, her hastiness and attitude can make even the best of men fall to their demise. I would not become one of them."

"Father, you know what must be done."

R'akl nodded.

"Saban Jai, I hereby place you under arrest."

Two Micran guards entered the room and stood beside Saban. R'akl commanded them to take Saban to the cell, but they refuse. Removing their helmets and presenting themselves as Warriors to Saban's cause. They raised up their swords and wetn to strike R'akl. Tartarus intervened and deflected the blows with two swords of his own. Saban ran out of the throne room as Serai moved beside Lola as they went and stood by her father as Tartarus commanded them both to leave and find safety.

Outside, the city is quickly placed under lockdown by Saban's warriors. In the streets stood Celedians and Micrans. Both on opposite sides as the Taranopolis civilians ran into their homes and evacuated themselves from the streets and open roads. Lola, Serai, and her father ran into one of the king's studies and locked the doors. At the palace, Saban stood at the balcony, overlooking the city and seeing his armies on the streets confronting the Celedians with their swords and spears. He grinned at the sight of it. Change appeared imminent.

"This day will prove that I am the new king of Argoron. The conquest is nigh."

In the desert, Porter continued to hear the voices coming through the waterfall. He slowly placed his hand in the water, feeling its coolness. Behind the waterfall seemed to be a cavern. From there, Porter placed his head through the waterfall and what he saw inside the cavern was a bright, spherical light.

"A wormhole."

He stepped into the cavern and approached the wormhole. Gazing inside, Porter began to make out an image. Looking closer as the seconds passed. Porter saw within the wormhole was a facility. Still looking, he recognized several vehicles parked. Porter's eyes widen.

"Area 51. Earth."

Seeing he was standing at the door, Porter took one step forth and-

CHAPTER 10: THIS IS ARGORON

Taranopolis is set between two forces as its civilians have fled into their homes and other nearby buildings. All in the fear of what's before their eyes. In the streets of the city, the Micrans and Celedians stood facing one another. Each of them wielding swords, spears, staves, and maces. Micrans even held shields as they stepped in the front of the face-off. Saban remained on the balcony, overseeing the two armies.

"This day, my warriors will overcome these savages and the city will thank me. Everyone will thank me."

Saban grabbed a bow and arrow from the table and set the arrow into one of the firepots on the balcony. He aimed smoothly and fired a shot into the middle of the armies. They saw the arrow pierce into the sand. The Micrans gazed up to the balcony, seeing Saban. From there, they yelled and charged toward the Celedians with force. Seeing the Micrans coming, the Celedians rallied themselves and ran into the fight with both forces colliding with weapons and shields.

Meanwhile as the battle commenced, R'akl remained inside the study with Lola and Serai. He hung his head, sulking in the shame of having such favor in Saban, only to have been betrayed. Lola informed her father that all will be well and once Saban is gone, they can continue on in life. R'akl took note of his daughters' words and yet, he continued to say that a king must rule Argoron. It is the natural law of the planet and the balance of their faith. Lola did not argue. She understood everything well. From the doors bolted in Tartarus, calming them down from his sudden appearance.

"Where is Saban?" R'akl asked.

"I do not know." Tartarus answered. "He fled from the throne room as soon as the fighting began."

"He's still here." Lola said. "He wouldn't have fled the city. He wants to look like the victor once the fighting has ceased."

"Then we must find him." Tartarus said.

"Go." R;akl said. "find Saban and bring him to me. He will face a swift justice."

"And what if he refuses to come alive?" Lola asked.

R'akl sighed and waved his hand. Lola nodded, looking back to Tartarus. The Celedian king understood the king's answer without a word and left the study.

On the streets, the Micrans and Celedians are slaughtering each other. Spears impaling, swords slashing, and shields deflecting. Some Micran warriors jointed into units of two and ambushed several Celedians who's heights exceeded even the average ones. Saban continued to watch as Tartarus searched for him throughout the palace. Lola sat with Serai and whispered something in her ear as she stood up and went for the door.

"Where are you going?" R;akl asked.

"To find Saban."

"Without someone to accompany you?"

"Tartarus is out there. I'm sure he'll be with me."

"Watch yourself out there."

Lola nodded with a smile as she headed out for Saban.

Saban grabbed a chair and sat down, overseeing on the

ongoing slaughter. He smirked, eating fruit and drinking wine. Standing behind him were two servants. Servants he rallied from within the city and stand with him as they watch the battle. Saban promised them greater positions under his rule. Bolting into the balcony behind was Tartarus with his sword drawn. Saban jumped up in a surprise fashion.

"Who let a savage into the upper floors?!"

"Only a fool would seem to find you on the streets in battle. Yet, you choose to watch like a worthless king."

"I am a king! Look down there! Your warriors are falling to mine. This day, you shall bow before me!"

"Oh no, betrayer. My warriors are known to overcome any amount of forces that appear before them. Your warriors will disobey your commands. For you are not their king."

Saban paused himself, his eyes glanced down toward the edge of the balcony where his sword rested. He jumped for the sword as Tartarus slammed his sword down, breaking the furniture as Saban slid on the marbled floor, grabbing his sword. He raised it up just as Tartarus' own clashed with it. The servants left the balcony and Saban grinned.

"A fight you want?"

"How else can your warriors see you for the false king you truly are."

Saban yelled, jumping on his feet and swinging his sword. He and Tartarus fought on the balcony as the fighting in the streets continued. Lola walked through the palace in search for Saban. She arrived outside, seeing the fighting in front of her. Blood spilling from the dead warriors. One of the Micrans ran toward her, beaten and bloodied. The warrior begged to hear word from her father. She had no reply as he warrior returned into battle. Hearing the clashing of weapons. She noticed the sound of clashing coming form above. Stepping out on the steps, Lola glared up to see Tartarus and Saban fighting.

51

"Oh no."

She moved with speed to reach the balcony as they continued fighting. Saban gained the upper hand on Tartarus by tripping him and he hanged on the edge. Saban grinned.

"Let's see if a Celedian can survive such a fall."

Tartarus went for a swipe, only to be kicked by Saban off the balcony, breaking the edge. The armies paused as Tartarus fell to the ground. Saban looked down at Tartarus' body. He smiled and made his way down, using a rope attached to his waist armor. Tartarus was still breathing, only in pain. Saban cocked his head, placing his foot over the Celedian King's body and looking out at both armies.

"I am your king now!"

The Micrans paused themselves in confusion. Seeing Saban wielding the sword in the air. The Celedians were more concern with their king's condition. Lola had made it to the balcony, only to see the broken edge and both Tartarus and Saban on the ground. Saban commanded both armies to bow before him and neither obeyed. Sensing their opposition, he yelled again, commanding them to bow. They did not bow.

"I am your king! King of Taranopolis! King of Argoron. My marriage to Princess Lola Arribel makes me your king!"

"Yet, we are not married yet." Lola said from above.

Saban turned around, gazing up. He grinned.

"Ah. The feat I have accomplish this day grants us our marriage and my ruler-ship as king. Who else could have taken out the Celedian king. The king of savages!"

"Did you kill him?" Lola asked.

"He's barely dead. Little close I'm afraid."

"You'll pay for this."

"By who's hand? Your father's?"

"No." A voice replied from the streets.

Saban looked out as did the armies. Lola saw who was

standing and a large smile formed upon her face. Tartarus' eyes looked up to see and he was pleased. Saban stepped off of Tartarus' body to confront him. Porter had returned.

"You come here uninvited?'

"I am." Porter said.

Saban chuckled, stepping down the stairs to face Porter. He looked him in the eyes and scoffed, backing up in his steps and raising up his sword.

"You think you can defeat me?"

"I know I can."

"That right?"

"Yes."

Porter raised up his sword and whipped the chain. Saban saw the chain and rubbed his chin. Impressed with Porter's choice of weaponry.

"Must be a Jagoron skill."

"You'll find out."

Saban screamed as he charged toward Porter with his sword. Porter deflected the attack and whipped the chain across Saban's back, cracking the armor. Saban paused, trying to look back at the armor. Porter nodded as Saban ripped the armor from his torso.

"I do not need the armor to defeat you."

Saban swung the sword several times, hitting Porter's own with Porter kicking Saban in the knee and tripping him on the sand. Porter yelled for Saban to stand up and continue fighting. Saban flipped himself up and ran after Porter. From there, Porter used the chain and grab Saban's sword. Snatching it from his hand and slicing his chest. Saban fell back as Porter stood over him with the sword in front.

"Do you yield?"

Saban chuckled, wiping the blood from his face.

"I'm not finished here. I am king."

"You are NOT King!" said R'akl standing behind him.

The Micrans saw him and instantly bowed before him. The Celedians had already went over and aided their king. Lola turned to her father before looking out at Porter and Saban.

"Stand back." R'akl said.

Porter nodded, stepping back from Saban as he stood up and turned to face R'akl.

"You have betrayed me, Saban Jai and I will not tolerate it."

"King R'akl, I was to marry your daughter. I was to be king."

"No. You are not king and you will no longer marry my daughter."

"This is not how Micrans do business!" Saban yelled. "You're disobeyed ancient Argoronian laws by this decision."

"I am king. Seems you have forgotten."

Saban looked out at the Micrans, seeing them bowed before R'akl. He looked around at everyone as anger brewed within him. Turning back to R'akl in anger. He had enough.

"I will not tolerate this any-"

R'akl took the staff he carried and swung it across Saban's head, breaking his neck. Saban's body fell into the sand and R'akl stood tall.

"A swift justice is done."

Lola approached Porter, amazed by his return.

"You thought I was leaving?"

"I did and how come you chose not to?"

"There's something here. Something calling to me. I'm not sure as to what it is. But, this planet, it needs my help. My world will heal itself. This one needs help now."

R;akl approached Porter, measuring him and looking at his daughter. He nodded with a smile.

"The decision is done." R'akl said.

"What decision?" Porter asked, looking over to Lola, who's smiling.

"For the protection of this kingdom and this planet, you will marry my daughter."

Porter nodded. Looking over to Lola. R'akl held out the staff and Porter placed both hands upon it. Lola had done the same. It was at that moment the two were married. The Micrans stood up and applauded them as the civilians came out of their homes to see the two. The bodies on the streets were cleared out and a ceremony was set the following day for Porter and Lola. He two had married just as Tartarus and R'akl came to an understanding. Tartarus left with the Celedians as Porter and Lola spent their honeymoon together.

During the night of the honeymoon while Lola slept, Porter was awake and walked out onto the rebuilt balcony, overseeing the city of Taranopolis. He smiled. Turning back to go inside, a voice called to Porter from the balcony. A strange one. Porter turned back to find himself facing an entity. Made of complete light. A bright white light. The light even had arms, legs, and a head.

"What are you?" Porter asked.

"I've been watching you since you arrived."

"Watching me? For what purpose?"

"A greater kind of purpose."

"And you are?"

"I... am a God of Argoron."

NEW ORDER OF THE WORLD: AN EVERWAR UNIVERSE SHORT STORY

A corridor confined with metallic walls. Silent. Streams of white smoke emit from the steel-plated floors and ceiling. Down the hallway, the echoing sounds of tapping. The tapping morphed into beating and through the smoke a young man who is called Timothy. Dressed in all black with a long sleeve shirt and jeans. Wearing boots. Timothy is sweating and is running in the sight of fear. His life at the present moment is depending on his speed. Behind him we see four silhouettes after him. The silhouette later manifest into a guard. They're known as the Realm Guards. Soldiers of the City and loyal to their leader. Donned in black armored uniforms, carrying high-powered artillery firearms diverse from single ranges to plasma-ranges, weapons similar to the rainshockers of the Viper Realm. Their faces shrouded by their black masks and goggles. Resembling reapers. No emotion can be seen from them. They chase down Timothy through the corridor. Timothy keeps running and stops at a nearby room. He enters the room as quickly as he could run. Timothy took a small moment to catch his breath. Though, he can still hear the footsteps of the guards coming near the room. Timothy looked around and found himself in the presence of a robot. The robot is modeled after human structure, equipped with the A.I. from the technologies in the land. The name of the robot is A14-12.

"You appear to be in a rush."

"The Realm Guards are after me." Timothy said, catching his breath. "I need to get rid of them."

"Now why would I assist you?"

"To keep them from killing me."

The robot examined Timothy and his garments.

"You're one of them."

Timothy nodded quickly. A14-12 recognized his intentions.

"Give me a moment."

Timothy waits for A14-12 to assist him, hearing the footsteps of the guards growing. Inching near him. Sweat drops from Timothy's forehead.

"They're coming closer!"

"Have some patience with me. After all, your kind know of patience."

A14-12 approaches Timothy with a device. The robot hands it to him. Timothy looks at it, unknown to what it is. He looks over at A14-12, questioning.

"What is this?" Timothy waved.

"If you want to evade the guards, hold it above your head."

Timothy scanned the device. Intrigued by its design.

"Is this some kind of teleporter?"

"No. They don't place them within this room. What you're holding will be good enough for your sudden cause."

The guards are near as their voices can be heard in the distance. Timothy holds the device above his head. A silver-colored mist fell from the device around him. Timothy notices himself becoming transparent. His flesh vanishing before his eyes. He knows he's becoming invisible. The guards burst into the room. Guns in hand. They circle the room, seeing only A14-12 standing. Calm demeanor for a robot. One guard approaches him. Eyes locked on tight.

"Mechroid, have you seen an enashian run past here?"

"I have not. You're the first I've seen this day."

"If you encounter the enashian, alert the Highguard."

"I will do that."

The guards leave the room and move further down the corridor. A14-12 looked around, scanning the room. Through the scanning process, the robot could see the invisible Timothy standing against the wall.

"Ah. There you are."

The robot grabbed a small firearm from the table and fired an electric bolt toward Timothy. The bolt hits Timothy in his left knee. He jolts and becomes visible again with the electric currents revealing himself.

"Why did you do that?!"

"You didn't make yourself visible, so I had to do it."

Timothy shook his head with a slight nod.

"Thanks."

Its not a problem. But, since you're here and finding your way out of this land. I assume you're on your way to finding the other renegades.

"The others?" Timothy jolted, waving his hands in disagreement. "No. No. I'm just trying to get out of this place with what I know."

"But, you're an enashian."

Timothy paused . The mechroid is aware Timothy isn't understanding the meaning of his words.

It's better of you to find them. You can lead them here to save the enashians and mechroids from the tyranny we live under.

"Why are you so interested in all of this?"

"I have my own reasons."

Timothy takes it in. Seeing what appears to be some form of character within the robot. A care perhaps? Unsure as to where the renegades may be.

"I'm on my way out of here anyway." Timothy let out a faint sigh. "I'll try to find the renegades."

"Maybe they'll find you."

"I'll take your word for it."

Timothy walks toward the door.

"We'll see once I get back. If I make it back."

"You'll be well." A14 said with certainty.

Timothy had left the room, running through the corridor and finding the exit. He exited the corridor and continued running.

Timothy runs outside of the base, he looks around, seeing himself surrounded by techno-buildings and flying drones made of beaten down metals. The buildings were as tall as skyscrapers and the air was lukewarm. The sounds of an electrical howling can be heard roaming in the skies above him. The city itself was one with great heaviness and astounding beauty. The structure looked to have been built many years ago. The aging itself had no greater effect than to instill fear. Its scent was of a burning fire mixed with electricity and a strange catch of cinnamon. He could hear the faint, yet squealing sounds of humans screaming coming from within the city. Their screams were of torment. It irked him, making his escape and finding himself entering the wilderness.

Timothy walks through the wilderness, known to those around the area as the Desolate. Nothing can be seen but a vast desert. Sand and rocks sit in places. Trees little to none. Few cactuses stood apart form each other. Scattered. Timothy walks through the Desolate as the wind slowly picks up and dust flies through the air. Timothy covers his face with his arm to avoid having sand fly into his eyes, nose, and mouth. He keeps walking as the wind increases in strength. The heat has increased in temperature and it begins to tire Timothy out. Yet, he continues moving through. After walking several more feet from his previous location, Timothy appears to spot a small structure up ahead.

"Is that a base?" Timothy glared.

As he goes to take another step, Timothy is stopped and lassoed from behind. Timothy looks down at the lasso around his torso. Hearing what is someone running toward him from behind, he turns his head, only to see a fist flying towards him. The fist punches Timothy, knocking him unconscious. Timothy awoke with a jolt. Beginning to regain his senses. Now knowing he's sitting down and his arms tied behind the chair. He's aware he's sitting in the middle of a room. The room is dark and the only light source he can see is coming from the sun above him through a circular hole in the ceiling. The room, of what Timothy could see was dirty with the Desolate sand. It smelled of vehicular oil and sweat. Its odor bothered Timothy, but he kept himself focused. Timothy tried looking around the room, seeing no one. He questions the scenario. He's tied up, so there must be someone within the room with him.

"OK." Timothy looked around. "This is strange. Anyone in here?"

No sound of a reply returns to him. Timothy quieted himself. Taking in a breath.

"Hello! Is there anyone in here besides me?! I'm pretty sure there is!

Footsteps are heard in front of Timothy. Though, he cannot see who's walking as they are shrouded in the thick darkness surrounding him. The footsteps come closer and more footsteps are heard. They are surrounding Timothy and he knows it. Shaking around in the chair to set himself free. A voice comes through the darkness facing him.

"No need for you to do such a thing." A voice echoed.

Timothy stops shaking and stares into the darkness. Looking for the location of the voice. Squinting his eyes.

"Who's there? Speak again."

The footsteps are heard once more. Only this time, Timothy can see the boots coming into the light and after several more steps, Timothy can see the one who spoke to him. A middle-aged man. Rugged in appearance, wearing cargo attire with a sleeveless shirt with scruffy facial hair and a almost shaved head. The man was the leader of the Renegades.

"Here I am."

Timothy looked. Seeing Castle in front of him. From all around Timothy and Castle enter into the light the other renegades. About a dozen of them.

"As you can see, you're not alone."

"Why am I tied to this chair?"

"Few of the watch guards caught you roaming through the Desolate, alone. They believed you to be a shell for the realm guards. You're not one of them are you?"

"I am not one of them." Timothy replied.

"Your uniform represents the Realm. Therefore, it makes you a loyal subject to the Dictator."

Timothy gazed down at his uniform. He even looked around, scanning the renegades' own attire. He knew they could tell the difference between the ones who are aligned with the Dictator and those who are the renegades. The apparel of the renegades were cargo pants and militaristic vests. Both dirty and wet from water.

"I see your reasoning, Mr.?"

"Just call me Castle. I would like to know your intent of running through the Desolate alone."

"I was told that I could find you out here. Maybe convince you to help free the others trapped in the City."

"Is that right?"

"It is." Timothy glared at the Renegades. "I can guess by your questioning that you're the leader.

"I am. Been leading the renegades ever since the fall of our freedom came to pass.

"I can see they trust you."

"Damn right they can. Most of them I been with me through the battles. Lost friends and loved ones along the way. Yet, together we stand tall."

61

Timothy nodded. Castle searched him, seeing if he could learn Timothy's motives.

"Tell me why you're here? Honestly."

"I escaped the confines of the City and ran into the Desolate. That's how your watch guards spotted me. I was told to find renegades by a mechroid."

Castle looked intrigued. Crossing his arms.

"What kind of mechroid?"

"An espionage mechroid. Operated with the technology within the City."

"Did it have a name?"

"Yeah."

"Tell me its name."

"That's not important. I can attest to that."

Castle stared at Timothy. His arms steady. No movement and little emotion.

"Why?"

"Try me."

Timothy nodded.

"A14-12. That was its name."

Castle looked over at the other renegades. They turned and spoke to each other before Castle focused his attention back to Timothy. Timothy could see the seriousness in Castle's eyes. Castle bent down toward Timothy, looking him in the eyes. Timothy shook with a certain fear. Castle's presence was something to fear. Even some of the renegades feared him.

"Where is this mechroid now?"

"Still in the City."

Castle grinned.

"I'm not certain to take what you've told me as fact."

"It's all true. That's the only reason I'm in this chair right now!"

"The only question is how could we enter the City when it is guarded by their snipers?"

"I…" Timothy shook. "I know a way inside the City."

"No shit." Castle scoffed.

"What I meant to say is I can take you and your group to the City. Sneak into the city and we can free the others."

Castle shook his head. Timothy couldn't tell if he accepted or rejected what he had told him. Castle stood in front of Timothy and cocked his head.

"How can we trust you?

"You can trust me. I'm not a betrayer.

"We'll know eventually. But, right now, we'll make our move into the City. And you'll be leading us in."

Timothy jerked with haste. Rattling the chair.

"Me? I don't understand?"

I'm not giving you the opportunity of bringing myself and my soldiers into death."

Timothy paused himself.

"I see your reasoning.

"That's a good start."

Castle reaches on the side of his leg and pulls out a knife. Timothy stops moving as Castle takes the knife and cuts the ropes from Timothy and the chair. Timothy sighs with relief as he stands up slowly from the chair. Castle takes the knife and places it onto Timothy's throat. Timothy gulped.

"Because if you wrong us in any way. I will personally kill you. Do you understand?"

"I understand."

Castle smiled, placing the knife back into his pocket.

"Good to know."

Castle looks to the renegades. He nods with a smirk on his face. The renegades rally up and equip themselves with their weapons, ranging from energy guns, plasma grenades, knives, and energy-coated knives." Timothy sees them gathering their

63

weapons. Feeling uneasy as he's just walking through the area.

Outside of the base, the renegades are sitting on dirt bikes, preparing to ride off toward the Realm's City. Timothy himself gets onto a bike. Castle sees him on the bike and points at him.

"You get in the front!" Castle pointed outward.

"You and your soldiers have the firepower." Timothy replied. "Why do I have to be in the front?"

"Get your ass in the front!"

Timothy went and sat atop the bike in front of them. Castle gave the renegades the command to follow.

The renegades had reached the city. They paused for a moment and Castle turns over to Timothy. Pointing at the city. Glancing up to the skyscraper structure and moving crafts.

"Lead us in."

"Of course. Follow along quietly. Hide your bikes over near the walls. The guards rarely do searches on this side of the city."

"Hide the bikes." Castle commanded the Renegades.

The renegades leave their bikes next to the wall. The wall is made up of a mixture between bricks and titanium wiring. The wiring glowed various colors with electricity flowing through it. It appears as if it was meant to be a twisted, yet somewhat beautiful sight to outsiders. Timothy guided Castle and the renegades toward the location where he had exited the city during his escape. The surroundings were clear as Timothy opened the door and they entered into the corridor.

Castle walked behind Timothy while the other renegades watched every corner. Prepared to fire.

"I have to ask you, kid. Why are you involved in all of this?"

"It's all a mistake." Timothy answered.

"A mistake? Saving others from tyranny is no mistake."

Timothy stops and faces Castle. Castle reads his eyes. He

senses something within him. Hidden behind his outward visage.

"I see. You're a deserter."

Timothy took note and continued walking.

"You turned against the Realm and for good reason."

"I turned against them because of the destruction they plan to bring."

"They've always plotted destruction. It's nothing new."

"Be that as it may. It doesn't spare me from the death I will receive."

"Death is only a solution of theirs. To trigger fear. What you've done, whether it is out of cowardice or bravery, it's for a greater cause."

Timothy listened to Castle's words closely.

"Hope I don't screw it up."

"You won't. You've shown me enough to figure that."

Walking through the corridor slowly, Timothy returned to the room A14-12 was in. Timothy enters the room with a storming haste.

The electric room is the base for the City's primary grid system. The walls glowing with a bluish hue as the energy flows through the wiring. Timothy looks around the room, but A14-12 is nowhere to be seen. Castle enters the room and looks around. Seeing the amount of tech that sat within its walls.

Castle scanned the room entirely. His eyes keen to the doorways.

"Look at this stuff."

Timothy looked over toward Castle. Shaking his head. Castle doesn't understand what Timothy's problem is or what he's trying to say.

"What is it?"

"The mechroid isn't here."

"Maybe it went to help the others find a way out."

"Maybe."

Not finding the mechroid, Timothy led them outside of the electric room.

As they step out into the corridor, on the other end are realm guards. Staring down Timothy, Castle, and the renegades. Their energy guns are searing and buzzing. Prepared for fire.

"Well, I'll be damned. We have company."

One of the realm guards raised up his plasma-range.

"Renegades! You have one request. Surrender yourselves now and come with us to be questioned and judged."

Castle stood firm. Determined about his next move as were the Renegades.

"I'm not going anywhere with you."

"We will now respond in the proper circumstance."

Castle stood his ground with the renegades. The realm guards begin firing toward the renegades. They run across the corridor. Some enter the electric room. Castle fires back at the guards with the renegades. Flying energy blasts zooming across the corridor back and forth. Timothy ran out of the corridor and into another doorway, which led down into another corridor.

Timothy ran through the second corridor and as he reaches its end, he bumps into A14-12. Standing around the robot are humans, beaten and battered, looking to escape. Timothy smiled.

"Where were you earlier?"

"I was preparing to aid these people for escape."

"How would you get them out?"

"I knew you were coming back with the renegades."

"How?" Timothy asked.

"I have my ways."

Timothy nods and leads them out of the corridor and toward the exit. He opens the door and the people barge out of the corridor.

"Get away from this place as far as you can."

The people run outside and towards the Desolate. Timothy

and A14 return to the first corridor, where they can hear the echoes of firing energy blasts. Nearing the doorway, the blasts slowly cease and turn into silence. Timothy, hesitant to open the door, opens it anyway. Timothy and A14 enter the first corridor and within the corridor are dead renegades and dead guards. They look and see Castle with several other renegades exit the electric room. Castle smiles and laughs as he approaches Timothy and A14.

"Where did you go?"

"I helped A14 set some humans free." Timothy looked around. "I see that you've managed to take them out."

"As you can see, I lost some of my own. Enough as I can manage at the moment."

Timothy turned to A14 as did Castle.

"We must leave this place now. She's coming."

"Who's coming?" Timothy wondered.

Castle shakes his head looking at Timothy as they proceed to exit the corridor and return to the outside.

"You mean to tell me that you don't know who "she" is?"

Timothy stood confused.

"I don't know who A14 is talking about. Who is this "she"?"

"We must hurry."

"Who is she?" Timothy asked.

They approach the exit door and open it. Running to the outside of the City.

Running outside, they find themselves chased by drones and several realm guards. Castle sees it and isn't happy about it. His face twists with anger and haste.

"Damn!" Castle yelled.

"This isn't good."

"You don't say."

A14 starts to beep as they get on the bikes. The mechroid can sense someone approaching them near the realm guards. A14 knows of that peculiar presence.

"Here she comes."

"I'm asking, who is she?"

Castle turned to face the guards. It was there he saw her in the distance. The footsteps sounded rough against the dirt. With vigor.

"Look ahead, kid." Castle pointed.

Timothy looks and see her. A woman dressed in all grey. Her dark hair down to her shoulders. Her eyes glowing of emerald. He lips red as blood. Her countenance as wicked as one could read. She is the Dictator.

They ride off into the Desolate as realm guards approach the Dictator. Bowing before her presence.

"Should we pursue them, my Lady?"

"No need." The Dictator grinned. "Everything is in proper order."

The realm guards returned to the City while the Dictator stared, watching the bikes ride out further into the Desolate.

MARK PORTER AND THOSE OF ARGORON WILL
RETURN IN:

THE
GODS and MEN
OF
ARGORON

NEXT STORY COMING FROM THE
PRODIGIOUS WORLDS

RAIDERS OF
VANOK

ABOUT THE AUTHOR

Ty'Ron W. C. Robinson II is the author of several works of fiction. Including the *Dark Titan Universe Saga*, *The Haunted City Saga*, EverWar Universe, Symbolum Venatores, Frightened!, Instincts, and others. More information pertaining to the author and stories can be found at darktitanentertainment.com.

Twitter: @TyronRobinsonII

Twitter: @DarkTitan_
Instagram: @darktitanentertainment
Facebook: @DarkTitanEnt
Pinterest: @darktitanentertainment
YouTube: Dark Titan Entertainment